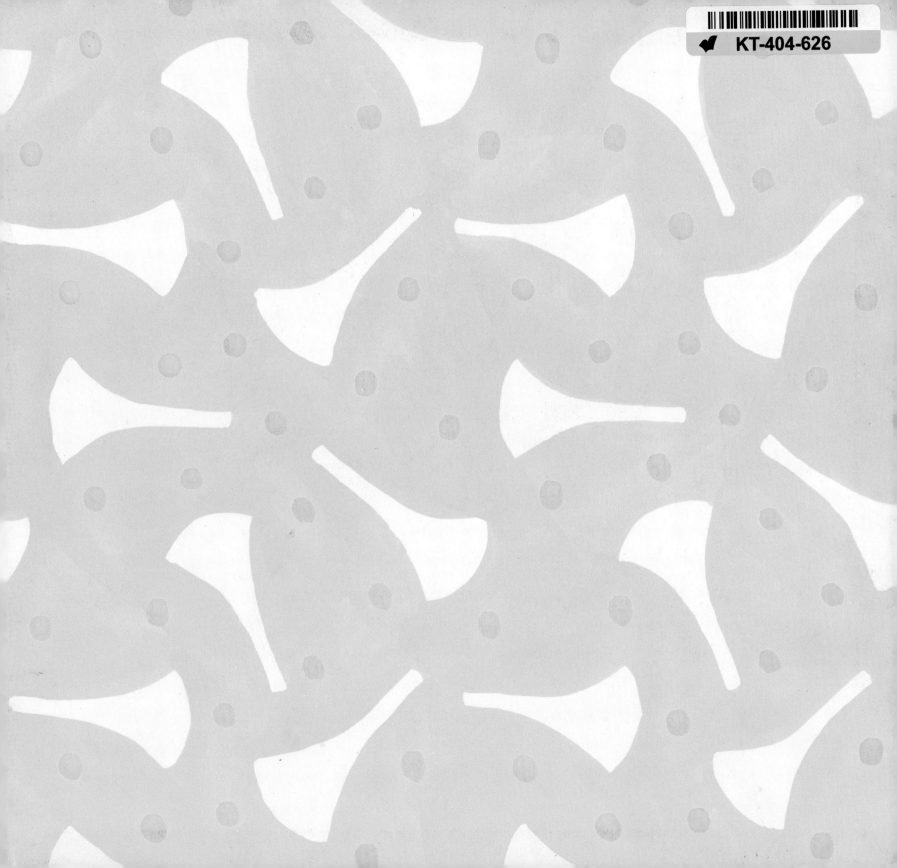

For Tom

First published 1995 by Walker Books Ltd
87 Vauxhall Walk, London SE11 5HJ

2 4 6 8 10 9 7 5 3 1

This book has been typeset in Kosmik.

Printed in Hong Kong

British Library Cataloguing in Publication Data
A catalogue record for this book is available
from the British Library.

ISBN 0-7445-4004-6

SEBASTIAN'S TRUMPET

Miko Imai

WALKER BOOKS
AND SUBSIDIARIES
LONDON · BOSTON · SYDNEY

It was the three little bears' birthday. Daddy and Mummy Bear had some special presents for them.

Theodore
got a drum.

Oswald
got a banjo.

And Sebastian
got a trumpet.

"Let's play
'Happy Birthday!'" they shouted.

And Sebastian
blew into his trumpet.
But the only
sound it
made
was

"What's happened to your trumpet?" asked Theodore. "Let me try it."

Theodore and Oswald
played "Happy Birthday"
for Daddy and Mummy Bear.

Rat-a-tat-tat

Twang

Twang

I wish I could play my trumpet, thought Sebastian.

Pfffffttt

"I HATE this trumpet!" Sebastian sobbed.

"Why did you give me a trumpet, Mummy? It doesn't even work!"

"Maybe you're trying too hard," said Mummy Bear. "Why don't you rest now and try again later?"

When Sebastian woke up, he couldn't wait to try his trumpet again. He tiptoed towards it.

TA-
OOOOON!
-TA-TA-
OOOOOOON!

And the three little bears all played
"Happy Birthday" together.

Rat-a-tat-tat

Twang

Twang

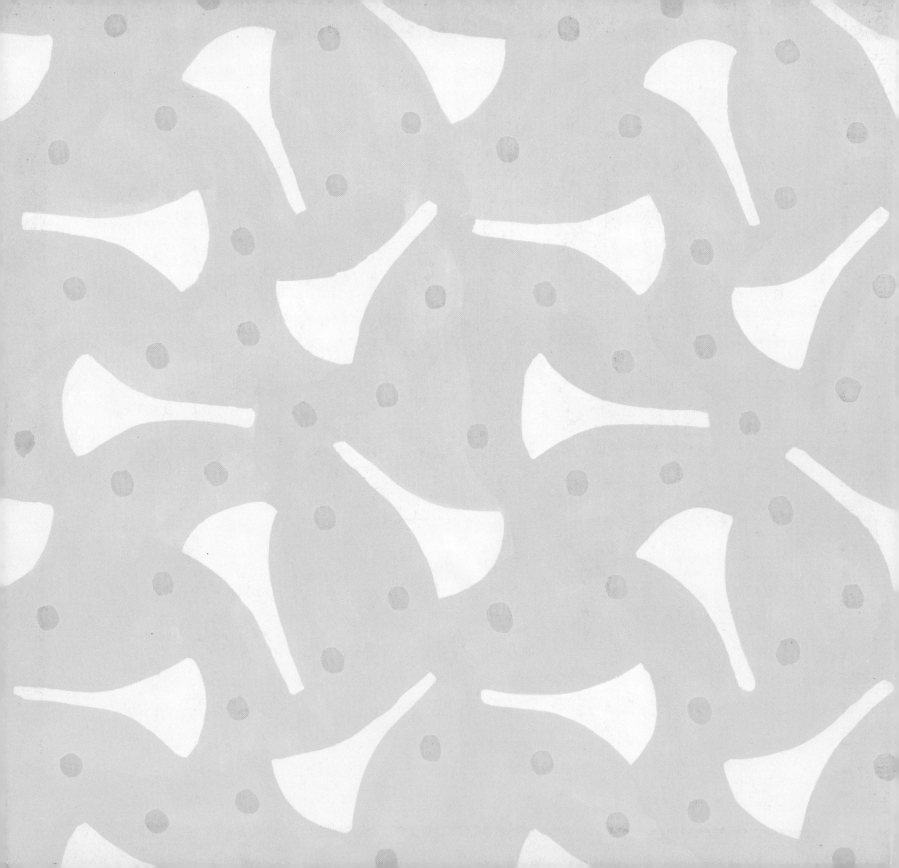